EVEN MOUNTAINS DIE

SCOTT BISHOP

Wanderlust Publishing House

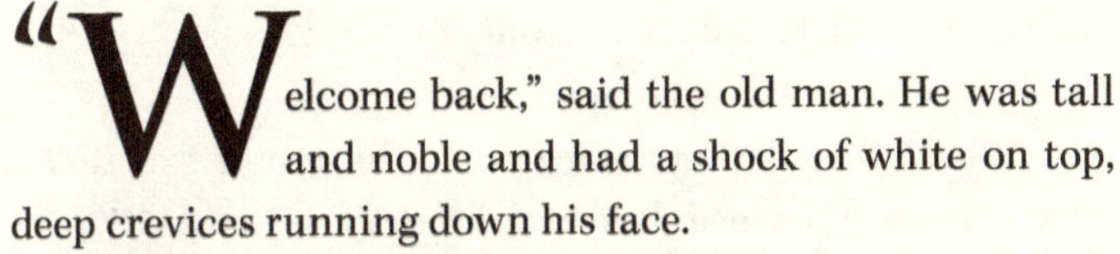

"Welcome back," said the old man. He was tall and noble and had a shock of white on top, deep crevices running down his face.

"Thanks. Wasn't planning on coming back so soon but...."

"You want to know," said the old man, completing the visitor's sentence.

"Yes. I want to know," conceded the visitor, quietly, seating himself on the ground. "I want to know where it's all headed."

"I understand. I cannot say."

"Why not?"

"Some secrets are best left secret. Knowing the future can have dangerous and unintended consequences. Only the sage can know the future without letting his knowledge affect his actions."

"But you know." Here, the visitor paused. "Tell me," he insisted.

A stiff breeze picked up. Gold and orange leaves, dark crimson ones, and leaves with curled brown edges, swirled on the ground, dancing to nature's time, gently crinkling, making music like small chimes swaying in the wind.

The old man peered through a canopy of trees, a kaleidoscope of colors beaming like stained-glass windows in an old stone church. The old man studied the deep blue sky. He sighed. "Alright. I will tell you what I know."

Choosing his next words carefully, speaking slowly and deliberately, the old man said, "I *see* the momentum lines. Thousands of them. Thinning out. They become five lines. Each holds an alternate possibility, a pathway to the future. The history you seek answers for is not yet written. Much needs to happen. Much needs to unfold before Humankind arrives at the doorstep of his annihilation...." Here the old man trailed off. Ending in a stronger voice, he said, "...or survival. The future is not complicated."

"The future isn't complicated?!" The visitor exclaimed. "That makes no sense. Just look around," he said. "We're a mess."

"True. Man has made a mess of his affairs. He fails to grasp the nature of life, of what is truly important. He chooses short term comfort over long term abundance. Profit over gratitude. Entitlement over compassion. He prefers earthly vices over quiet moments."

Puh! The visitor angrily spat on the ground. "Sorry," he said.

"No need to apologize," the old man interjected.

"I wasn't apologizing to you."

"Yes. I know."

"Then why tell me there's no need to apologize?"

"Because she knows it was not directed at her."

The two fell silent. Leaves performed cartwheels in front of them. The sun had risen above the horizon, and birds were chirping in trees, their bellies full from morning meals, as critters stirred from thistle and down nests, homes that had kept them safe and warm from autumn's first frost.

"Don't be too critical," said the old man. "You were once the way of many men."

"I was *never* that way," the visitor said, adamantly. "I was just caught up in it. Still am. To a degree. Never bought into their way. Never gravitated towards it. All I ever wanted was a small corner of this world, a place to call my own." The visitor hissed in a breath. "But this...this insanity, this...this...madness is impossible to escape...completely. A person has to survive."

"Still so much to learn."

The old man craned his neck upward. Through cloud covered eyes he studied the sky a second time.

"I see another. One that was not there before. A momentum line bypassing all the rest. A line sweeping the world down a path of hardship. There is much chaos on this one. Great destruction. Horrors. The end happens quickly. And here," said the old man tapping the sky, "here is another leading to devastation in a blink of an eye." The old man shuddered. "Both lines are feint, barely visible. They have not yet taken hold as strong possibilities."

The visitor sat staring at his mentor, the only sound leaves rustling in the wind. "Solomon," he said placidly, "what aren't you telling me?"

"For every step Man takes, for every time Man places his foot down upon the earth, Humankind either creates another line or breathes life into one that exists. It does not appear that Man is headed towards a desirable outcome. Should man take more steps in either of these new directions these feint lines will turn into strong, durable ones, real possibilities, lines capable of carrying the world down a path of annihilation. Swiftly."

"You sound as if our extinction is inevitable."

"It is not my young friend. Humankind can choose a

different future, a bright one." The old man paused as he scried the sky. "But they do little to ensure it."

"So you know. You *see*. You know where it's all headed," insisted the man.

"No I do not. Not even my sight can *see* such things," said Solomon. "All I can *see* is where Man is headed and where he has been, the momentum lines that form his past, present and future. The only one who knows where Man is headed is Man himself. Man chooses on which momentum line he wants to travel. He decides whether he wants a future of peace and prosperity or one of rage and conflict, and extinction. Man, alone, decides his destiny. Man can choose poorly or he can choose wisely. I have no control over his affairs. All I can do is sit, and wait...and hope. There is always that. Hope."

"Hope? You see hope in the momentum lines?"

"Yes. One fragile line bears Man's hope."

The two men were facing each other at Summit Rock, away from the winding pathways of the Mall and Ramble, the gardens, the loop around the lake too. A bright zephyr wrapped an easy cool around them. The sun, drying the last drops of dew from the grasses and damp from the leaves, began to spread his heat like a cozy blanket over the fields and meadows, and among the lawns and forests even as he stretched his delicate fingers down woodland trails and sprinkled sun-kissed radiance down trickling streams, waking this sleepy corner of the world to a new day.

"Did you bring the little men?" Solomon asked.

"Yes. They're right here in my pack. Wasn't going to bring them. Didn't see the point in it. You always win."

"Come now. Set the men up and move them as usual."

"Why bother Solomon. You're just going to beat me."

"You know that?"

"Of course I know that. You *always* beat me."

"Hmm, I do see your point," Solomon good naturedly quipped in his gravelly, baritone voice. He paused. Turning serious, he said, "Perhaps it is you who beat yourself."

"*Beat* myself?! How do I beat myself? You're the one who's always looking into the future and anticipating my every move."

"True. But that is how you explained the game to me, no? Defend. Attack. Anticipate your opponent's next moves."

"Solomon!" The man mildly rebuked his mentor. "The game wasn't meant to be played the way you play it."

"So many rules," chortled the old man.

"So many rules is right. You can't just go and change them."

"Why not?"

The man thought about this for a moment before saying, "Looking at the momentum lines, of the pieces, of outcomes, not to mention of your opponent, me, to see how I'll react to one of your moves. It's just not good gamesmanship."

"Details. Details."

"*So-lo*-mon...." the man said, beginning to lose his patience. "You...you won our first match together. How do I compete with that? That's not supposed to happen. There's no beginner's luck in this game. Only skill. Skill brought on by experience."

"Perhaps I am a child prodigy," the old man said, chuckling.

The visitor burst out laughing. "I'm serious," the man said, trying to keep a straight face.

"So am I," Solomon returned in a tone that makes a person sit up and take notice. "You lack faith."

The man gulped back the truth in his mentor's words.

"Are you sure you've never played before?" asked the man trying to change the topic.

"Positive. Never. Not until we met," said the old man, unequivocally. "You taught me all I know. Answer me this. Why do you limit yourself? Why not play the way I play? We are just two old friends playing a game not bound by any rules, least of all Man's."

"Look who's calling who old," the man chided his mentor.

Solomon sat, unmoved, waiting for an answer, appearing as though nothing less would do.

The man shifted uneasily. "I don't know why Solomon," he began. "Perhaps..." the man hesitated. "It's hard," he said, shaking his head. "Despite everything I've been through, everything I've *seen*, it's too incredible to believe. Heck. Sometimes when I step out of my shoes and think about it, when I stop to remember everything that's happened, there are moments I think I'm crazy."

"You are not crazy," the old man said. "Just because a truth lies beyond a man's comprehension, does not make it any less the truth."

"Since *you* know so much, why don't you explain why I don't win?"

"Confidence and doubt. You lack the former and have more than enough of the other. To say more is not my place."

The man heaved a sigh of exasperation. "Why must you talk in riddles all the time? Are we back to knowing the future and how the sage doesn't let his knowledge affect his actions?"

"Yes. I must not let my knowledge affect you."

"Why Solomon? Why all the cloak and dagger stuff? What would be so wrong if you told me?"

"I have explained myself. Knowing the future can have dangerous and unintended consequences."

"How so?" the man pressed.

"The sage leaves no tracks in the snow. He casts no ripple in the sea of time."

"Why not?"

Solomon looked at the man, smiled fondly and said, "It is not for me to write your story. You must write your own story. So must Man." The visitor was about to say something but the old man continued. "To say more is to attempt to manipulate the future. Your future. My future. Our future. The future is not up to me to decide. I am but a bit player among the stars of the Universe. If I were to strive to bring about a particular outcome, one that I would like to see...well, such uses of *power* never turn out the way you want them, no matter how well intentioned. You should know that better than anyone. To say more is to risk infecting our future. Just like Man must choose his own destiny, free from influence, free from interference from the likes of me and of others, you must choose yours."

"It's just a good thing I like you," said the man, completely exasperated, knowing his mentor would take the conversation no further. The man dug into his beat up backpack and pulled out a well worn wooden box. He unfastened the tarnished brass buckles that were keeping the box shut and flipped the lid up. Grabbing the pawns, the rooks and the other chess military he laid them out, white pawns in one row, black pawns in another, and in like fashion he organized the ranked pieces in rows according to color and strength, after which, he set the military up on a thick slab of granite.

"We are the same you and I. You have not accepted that yet," said Solomon.

"What color do you want to be?" the man asked, ignoring his friend's last remark.

"Black. You can have the advantage."

"Yeah, right. Some advantage. You ready?"

"Lay on McDuff."

"Shakespeare?! Where'd you hear Shakespeare?"

"Oh, you know," Solomon said, a hint of coyness in his voice. "The neighborhood. People talk. I listen."

"Uh-huh," the man looked at Solomon and, pushing a pawn two squares forward said, "King's pawn to e4."

"Again?" Solomon softly chastised. "You open the same way every time. How boring. Where is your creativity?"

"You going to talk smack or you going to play?"

"Very well. King's pawn to e5," yawned Solomon. The man stretched his hand across the board and, according to their arrangement, moved the pawn for his friend.

"King's knight to f3."

"Queen's pawn to d6," countered Solomon, the man moving the chess piece for him.

"My queen's pawn to d4."

"Queen's bishop to g4." Turning his attention away from the game, Solomon cast his *sight* out to read the unseen meridian lines around him. "Sheep Meadow is quiet. So is Strawberry Fields."

"What about the North Woods? And the Ravine?" the man asked, keeping his eyes glued to the chess board.

"Both...quiet," the old man said, returning back to the game.

The visitor looked up from the board and into the trees where sunlight dappled down. Rays, streaming through the leaves, landed playfully on his face, a warm medicine for the long walk he had taken to reach the old man. Noticing the morning for the first time, the man said, "It's gorgeous. You'd think there'd be more people out."

Reading the meridian lines again, Solomon said, "The day is early. They will come."

"My pawn at d4 captures your pawn at e5," said the man.

"Bishop to f3," said Solomon. The man leaned over and moved the piece, swiping the captured white knight off the board in one quick, fluid motion of his hand.

"Queen captures bishop on f3."

"Aggressive today," Solomon needled.

"Aggressive? You should talk threatening my Queen in three moves. What did you expect me to do, let you just take it?"

"I expected you to react in the manner you did. D6 to e5. You are down another pawn," stated Solomon.

"Thanks for the analysis," the man said, dryly, as he reached over and moved the pawns, one a square diagonally forward, the other taken off the board. "It's called development, Solomon. Sometimes you have to sacrifice a piece to develop your game."

"Is that what you did? You sacrificed your knight for the betterment of your game?" asked Solomon.

"No. Not exactly," the man mumbled. "I'm having a hard time concentrating. But sometimes you have to. Sacrifice a piece I mean. Sometimes a piece is in the way and you can't develop your game unless it's captured. Sacrificing a piece helps to clear the board so you're free to develop your strategy," explained the man. "It doesn't work on you though," the man sounded dejected. "You see what's happening before my game *ever* has a chance to develop."

"Answer me this," said Solomon. "How is the way I play any different from the way you play? We both play with strategy. No?"

"*Strategy*?! You call the way you play, playing with strategy. *You* cheat!" the man said. "King's bishop to c4," huffed the man.

Remaining stoic and calm, Solomon said, "Cheating is a matter of perception. Is my way not more efficient?"

The man offered no response.

"Queen's bishop to c5," called Solomon.

"My queen from f3 to b3."

"Queen's knight to c6," Solomon said. "Look. People come now."

The two friends paused to watch a young couple walk across a wide expanse of lush lawn — The Great Lawn as it was known — a sea of green grass ringed by mighty oak trees. The young pair frolicked and played, laughing until their stomachs hurt, twirling around like old-fashioned carousels, the kind you lean out from the horse on, way out, to grab a brass ring for a free ride. They spun around until they got so dizzy they could no longer hold each other up. They fell to the ground on top of each other, the sweet, soft grass cushioning their fall. Playing turned into touching and touching turned into kissing and kissing turned into caresses that prompt hungry mouths to feed upon each other. Entangled as one, their passions lit, the two fell deep into the earth, the Mother cradling them in her protective embrace. When they were through the man got up, bent down, and, grasping the woman's hands, pulled her to her feet. They straightened their clothes and without a care in the world, carried on, no one around the wiser or to bother their business. They walked across the field, passed a large boulder, and into the oaks disappearing from sight.

"Solomon, how can they walk by and just ignore you like that?"

"They do not ignore me. They might not pay attention to me in quite the same manner you do, but they do not ignore me, completely. True, they seem oblivious. They walk past me, hand in hand, as though I were not here. But that does not mean they do not take notice. They do, on a superficial level. They know I am here because they see me. Many are like these two taking little interest in me. But others? Others are different. Others have a deeper level of understanding, a far greater respect for their elders, and for those who are ancient among us. Few are as lucky as you."

"Yeah, right. I'm real lucky," the man said, sarcastically. "My bishop on c4 captures your pawn on f7. Check."

"Playing tough," said Solomon, hoping to incite the man further.

"Yeah, well, it's all about winning. Just like life."

"Is that what life is about?"

"Well, no. Not entirely. But it helps," said the man, determined to beat Solomon.

"King to e7. If you would do the honor."

"Gladly," stated the man moving the king. "Queen's bishop to g8. Check."

"King's knight to f6."

"Castle. Kingside."

"Such a tepid move," said Solomon. "Game over."

"What?" The man blinked. He was nearing his brink. "What do you *mean* game over?"

"Knight on c6 to d4," Solomon called.

"My queen moves from b3 to g3."

"So desperate," said Solomon, egging the man on, waiting for the man's temper to erupt.

"Keep playing Solomon," the man grumbled. "Keep playing."

Yawning again, the old man said, "My knight, d4 to e2."

The man moved Solomon's knight and studied the board, calculating the old man's next moves along with his. His king into the corner square, Solomon's knight capturing his queen. Check. His king back to the square it had moved from, black knight captures his rook. King captures knight, black queen clear across the board. Checkmate. Disgusted, the man silently groaned to himself even as a flicker of anger passed through his face, the frustration of another loss eating at him. "You think you have me in three moves, don't you?" he said.

"I do," smiled Solomon, knowing how his friend would react but not knowing, hoping he would take the bait.

Firm in resolve, the man sat, staring at the board, a scowl

on his face, clenching his hands and grinding his teeth, the muscles in his neck and jaw as taut as the skin of a drum.

Forcing himself to relax, he closed his eyes and willed himself to take deep breaths.

Tension trickled from his body.

He took several more breaths, deeper, cleansing ones as he emptied his mind.

More tension ran from his limbs.

The man's breathing, rising and falling in a hypnotic cadence — in, out, in, out — like waves lapping on the edge of a beach, began nudging him away from the shore of the world. His arms went limp, his legs too, and his chin came to a loll in the dimple of his neck. Aggression gave way to frustration, frustration gave way to calm, and calm surrendered to serenity. Behind closed eyes, the black of consciousness dissolved into a vivid world of gray even as the man's first body, his light body, softly disengaged from his physical one and floated through the veil that separated the physical world from the next. The trees around him, the grounds and the old man too, appeared in the palest version of gray, though some might say the color was a cloud white. The man had stepped into the twilight, the gray world, a quiet space where time has no meaning and where the impossible is merely improbable, a world where energy is alive and visible, and mutable.

Fully immersed in this parallel world, the man's attention came to rest on the chess board. The game, dressed in a symphony of grays — dark grays and light grays, of charcoal, of heather, of every imaginable hue — pulsed in the night. Kings and queens, bishops and rooks, knights and pawns appeared as throbbing gray lines. Knights jumped in all manner of directions, rooks and queens snaked across the board, bishops too, going forwards and backwards, over and under, looping and twisting, to the left and to the right, moving squares ahead and full across the board, and pawns, they moved in their slow trudging manner. Bishops captured knights, knights captured queens, rooks took out pawns, kings defended, kings attacked, every conceivable move was present, and a few unlikely ones too, the game was one, big knotted mess, glowing an ethereal gray, the beginnings and endings of the match a smoky fringe about the board's border.

The man sat, cross legged, in a trance, his light body firmly in the twilight, searching the myriad lines and the infinite possibilities they offered. He studied the future lines, the ghostly waving gray threads massed along the board's edges. There were so many it made finding what he was searching for a daunting task. The man knew what he was looking for though.

He plunged deeper into the twilight.

Solomon smiled.

Carefully, the man's eyes traveled about checkmate's border, methodically scanning the strands. Not finding what he was looking for, he retraced the board's edges, and traced them again.

When he could not find what he was looking for panic set in. His confidence faltered.

The twilight began to shimmer. The spectral world slowly lost its detail. Black slowly encroached upon the gray, the natural world lying a heartbeat away.

Sitting in the pitch dark, the man battled his resolve, alternating between unraveling his emotions and releasing them. Gradually, his breathing returned to the steady cadence that had led him to the twilight, and when he came upon the veil, he stepped through, the eerie, pulsing threads returning.

The man went deeper.

More filaments than before appeared.

He looked into the throbbing mass, searching the lines with care, until, in front of him, buried deep inside the pulse, barely visible, a gleaming thread of delicate silver twinkled. The man permitted himself a moment of self approval.

Coming closer to the line, being careful not to disturb the strand lest it dissolve into the twilight and be brushed out of existence forever, he traced the line to where the filament exited the board. Setting his intention, the man sent a puff at the spot, soft and slight, the kind that might come from a baby's mouth. Precious points of light, like dust glinting in sunshine, quavered in the twilight. The line glowed a speck brighter.

At the point where the line fell off the board and into his future, the man intended another puff, as gentle as his last. The strand received the man's breath, the thread glowing a smidgen brighter. Checkmate, saw the man.

The man sent another well intentioned puff into the line, slightly stronger than the last, and saw Solomon's knight capturing his queen. The man puffed on the line again, stronger still, the strand revealing his queen moving full across the board placing Solomon's king in check. The man continued tracking the filament, backwards, sending gentle puffs into the line along the way. With each breath, his intention added life to its reality. And his confidence grew.

With deep, abiding intention, he sent another breath towards the strand. The filament reverberated, twinkling silver.

Yet another puff revealed the game at its inception.

Confidently, the man sent his intention at the point the strand entered the board. The tip flared a brilliant silvery white, momentarily. And as it did, he saw his first move and Solomon yawning. He saw his knight come out followed by a black pawn. He saw Solomon's bishop threatening his queen and the flurried exchanges of white pawn for black pawn, bishop for knight, queen for bishop. He continued tracking the line forward until he saw the decision that had sent him down the dark gray path of defeat.

Stealing himself, fighting every instinct he had, he breathed intention into the branch not taken. The strand glowed pale silver, just for a moment, before fading back to gray. He sent his intention along the line again. The thread regained its silvery cast, holding on to the hue, neither advancing nor retreating.

Again he breathed his intention along the entire length of the line, from beginning to end. The thread lit up like the silver of a star at midnight. The man could see the full details of the game now. He studied the sequence of game winning moves, paying special attention to how Solomon would react. As he memorized the game, the line grew stronger, so too its color. Confident he knew the match by heart, the man, now bold and certain of the outcome, sent his breath along the entire length of the strand one last time. The line shone in a shocking star white brilliance and as it did, the man took the thread, fully strong, fully developed, now a hardened reality, and gently, with his fingers, pulled its essence into his heart.

Solomon watched in silent approval.

"Bishop to f3," said Solomon. The man leaned over and moved the piece, swiping the captured white knight off the board in one quick, fluid motion of his hand.

"Queen captures bishop on f3."

"Aggressive today," Solomon needled.

"Aggressive? You should talk threatening my Queen in three moves. What did you expect me to do, let you just take it?"

"I expected you to react in the manner you did. D6 to e5. You are down another pawn," stated Solomon.

"Thanks for the analysis," the man said, dryly, as he reached over and moved the pawns, one a square diagonally forward, the other taken off the board. "King's bishop to c4."

"My king's knight to f6."

"Queen from f3 to b3."

"My queen to e7," said Solomon. "Look. People come now."

The two stopped their game to watch a young couple walk across a wide green lawn ringed by mighty oak trees. The lovers frolicked and played, laughing until their sides hurt, running in large circles, playing catch me if you can, the young woman teasing and taunting her male suitor, daring him to take her in the grass. Every time the young man came within arm's reach and was about to claim his prize, the woman would slip away putting a good distance between the two only to coax her partner to take the chase up once more. When the woman did allow the man to catch her, they were by a boulder, thrice as tall as a man, a coincidence having been neatly arranged by her. With the chase now over, she turned the tables on him, pinning her partner against the rock, devouring him with hungry kisses. Out of breath and caught off guard, the man could do little except submit as the woman clawed his shirt off and tore at the buckle on his belt. The two kissed, frantically, as the woman pawed at the man pulling his remaining clothes off. Then she led him behind the rock.

When they were through, the man, fully spent, sheepishly peered around the boulder. Satisfied no one was watching, he signaled to his paramour that the coast was clear. They retraced the trail of their carnal desires, hurriedly picking up their garments from where they had fallen. They tossed their clothes on, straightened themselves out and, without a care in the world, carried on, no one around the wiser or to bother their business. They walked across the field until they passed under the oaks and were lost from sight.

"Queen's knight to c3," said the man.

"Pawn to c6," countered Solomon as a strong gust of wind, straight as an arrow and as sharp as a knife, whistled in low sending the black pawn ahead one square. "What troubles you?" Solomon asked, as three sentries sitting in a nearby birch jovially cawed, sharing the old man's move between themselves. "You did not come all this way just to learn where Man is headed."

"No. No I didn't," the man admitted, scratching his head, eyeing his friend suspiciously from beneath a furrowed brow. "Queen's bishop to g5," he said. "I wanted company."

The man started to say something but stopped. He looked down at the chess board and then at Solomon, trying to find words for what he wanted to say next. He opened his mouth but nothing came out.

The man stared into the trees.

Minutes passed. Solomon patiently waited.

"I've *seen* too much," the words tumbled out the man's mouth so softly they were barely a whisper.

"Yes. You have," Solomon agreed, paused, then offered. "*Seeing* is the beginning of wisdom."

Turning his face to meet Solomon's, the man shook his head saying, "I don't understand."

"It is what a man does with what he *sees*, and the knowledge he gains from his *sight* that makes a man wise. A man can walk a thousand lifetimes with knowledge at his side, but if he abuses his knowledge, mis-uses it in any way, it will never be said that he walked the earth with wisdom."

"Knowledge, wisdom," the man scoffed, pitching a stone against the base of an oak tree. "Neither help me. How do knowledge and wisdom help me get ahead in life?"

"Knowledge and wisdom do not advance a man's life. Knowledge and wisdom advance a soul's life. And one soul is all it takes to make a difference."

"Who cares, Solomon?" groaned the man. "I don't fit in this world."

"Yes. You feel this way," Solomon said, patiently. "You have felt different from the moment you arrived. I have seen this in you. From the day you entered this world, you have been searching for a place to call home among your kind."

"I don't belong here. Not in this world anyway."

"You belong in this world far more than the next man. Man, he leads us down a path of great tragedy," said Solomon, bitterly.

"But I thought...you said...."

"I should not speak so critically of Man," Solomon cut the man off, correcting himself. "Not all men are alike. Not all men are equal. There are a few." Here Solomon stopped, his words hanging in the air.

The sun had topped the trees and was reaching for the sky even as the last remnants of the morning chill settled deep into the ground. People were out wandering the Mall, the Ramble, Sheep Meadow and Strawberry Fields, and a father and son were fishing on the Lake. A few intrepid souls, they could be seen cutting through the North Wood on their way to The Ravine.

"It's like you said, we seek profits over gratitude, entitlements over compassion, we're in it for the short term," said the man. "My world is a world of part time values and full time lies. We accept and practice our values but only if they're convenient to follow. We're short on integrity." Here the man stopped. He looked straight at the old man and asked in a desperate voice, "Why can't people see Solomon? Why don't they get it?"

The old man looked at his friend, kindness in his eyes. When he looked away, the warmth in his face had snuffed out replaced with a burning anger. He took a deep breath and spat, "Money. Money has doomed Man since the beginning. Money has doomed us all."

The man adjusted himself, sitting closer to his mentor. "Solomon. I've never heard you this way."

"Pay me no mind," Solomon said, looking at the man. "I am but a foolish old man."

Concern for his friend etched on his face, the man softly asked, "Why give us money at all?"

"Man was not given money. Man created money himself."

"Why?"

"To facilitate trade between himself."

"Sure. That makes sense."

"Yes. But Man soon learned money set himself apart from his own kind," Solomon replied. "The more he had, the more resources he could command. The more resources he could command, the more power he had. The more power he had, the more his fellow Man looked to him. It did not take long before money and power became synonymous with being able to control one's fate. Such a foolish idea."

The man nodded his head in agreement. "Power. Prestige. Money. They're the three currencies of the world today."

"They have been the currencies of the world since the dawn of modern Man," said Solomon.

"Money rules them all though," the man said. "If you have enough money, it'll buy you all the power and prestige you want. And where there's money, corruption isn't far behind."

"Do not forget beauty and youth, my friend. The Gods and Angels gave Humankind beauty and youth to take down men of great power when the imbalance between men with power and men without becomes too great. Beauty and youth are apt seducers. For the powerful, they can be impossible to resist."

"You're right," agreed the man. "Beauty and youth are powerful seducers. Beauty and youth can be leveraged into money, princely sums of it." The man thought for a moment before adding, "But beauty and youth are depreciating assets."

"Yes. Beauty and youth are fleeting," Solomon said. "It is as it was decided upon long ago."

A quiet settled between the friends. They watched people meander about, enjoying the autumn day. The sky had turned a deep, rich blue, an occasional puffy, white cloud chugged across it. A gentle breeze whispered through the trees. Wrens, jays and other birds flitted from one branch to the next while squirrels and other animals foraged for what berries and nuts they could find.

"Poverty," said the man thinking aloud. "Poverty is a prison as real as a jail cell."

"Yes," agreed Solomon. "But wealth has its shadow side. Wealth builds walls around those who have it. Wealth makes a man sleepless at night."

"Maybe. But without money a man has no mobility. A man is stuck with the circumstances he is born into," asserted the man. "A man with money can buy a car, a ticket that will take him somewhere, he is able to move about. I'd rather live in the citadel wealth builds than be shackled in the dungeon of poverty."

The conversation was at a stalemate.

With a soft look in his eyes, the man gazed at the chess board, a chipmunk twittering a few feet away. Paying it no mind, the man went deep inside himself, returning to the threshold that had led him to the gray world. With his body relaxed, his mind quiet, and his breathing rhythmic, he stepped into the twilight, and studied the ghostly pulse lying on top the board. Glowing a brilliant star silver, he quickly found the thread he was seeking. He tracked the filament, from beginning to end, reacquainting himself with the moves that lied ahead.

Stirring the man from his trance, an amused Solomon said, "Pawn to b5."

"Whah? Yes, of course. Your pawn to b5," mumbled the man, moving the piece. "My knight captures your pawn."

The chipmunk, wide-eyed with wonder, curious about the strange army of men that had sprung up in the middle of nowhere, scurried up to the edge of Solomon's side of the board. The two men sat watching the animal, giving the critter its space. The chestnut striped rodent sniffed to its left where Solomon's king stood, and then to its right where another piece sat. After deeming the area safe, the chipmunk gingerly tested the empty ground before him. The stone felt sturdy enough.

Curiosity claiming the better of the animal, the critter looked left and then to its right and, all at a once, without knowing why, leaped onto the board, its feet and hands landing full on the board all at once. The chipmunk tested the ground again. Feeling secure, it widened its search. The animal sniffed the piece in front of the king, first down, then up, and when it came to the crown, one of its five obsidian pearls poked its nose, startling the creature, causing it to jump backwards clear off the board. After collecting itself, and with a little mystic urging, the chipmunk braved forward once more. This time the chipmunk carefully avoided the crowned couple keeping instead to the empty space directly in front of it.

With its head lowered, its nose and whiskers twitching, the chipmunk came to the base of a black piece that came roughly up to its own small shoulders. The chipmunk sniffed the pawn. The critter, having nosed its way around half the pawn's circumference, came upon a piece of considerable heft and size sitting on an adjoining square. Finding this piece more interesting than the pawn, the chipmunk began exploring, sniffing its circular base and then its upper body. When it came upon its face, the small animal was surprised to find a snout not so unlike its own which got the animal thinking it had come upon another of its kind.

The chipmunk stood on its feet and rested its tiny hands on the knight's face. But the horse didn't budge, not even a twitch. The chipmunk patted its front paws on the knight's face. When the chipmunk got no reaction, the critter tapped all the harder and leaned its weight against the piece sending the two toppling over.

Trying to keep a straight face, Solomon said, "Pawn at c6 captures your knight."

The three sentries flapped their wings applauding the old man, cawing, cheering him on.

"Uh hm," replied the man, eyeing his mentor. "Bishop at c4 takes the pawn you captured my knight with."

"I have seen Man do terrible things for money," said Solomon. "Money emboldens Man to take more than his comfortable needs. His appetite is not easily satisfied. Queen's knight to d7," called Solomon.

"Castle. Queenside."

"A long time ago," continued Solomon, "men in togas and sandals, a modern, civilized nation for their time, had their senate and emperors. Powerful men whose only desire was to sit with the good fortune life had bestowed upon them. They held their positions as long as the populace remained happy. That was simple. The masses were easily pacified with games and food. 'Give them their bread and circuses,' was how they justified themselves. Justification for crossing a sea and invading the fertile lands to their south. Justification for taking what was not rightfully theirs. Queen's rook to d8," said Solomon.

"Rook from d1 captures your knight at d7," said the man.

"And not so very long ago, men from a distant shore helped free this land. These men threw their support behind this fledgling nation to ensure that their brothers, men who lived on an island to their north, would not become more powerful and wealthier than their own kingdom. But their spending left their nation on the brink of collapse, and a time of great hardship followed. Drought yielded poor harvests. Their animals incurred disease. The cost of bread became too expensive except for a fortunate few. The poor became resentful. Desperation gripped the cities and countryside. Unrest spread among the poor. The rich, they imposed taxes on those who could least afford to pay yet failed to provide abundance to those who needed it most. Years went by, as did one financial crisis after another. Discontent and political corruption ruled the land, until the poor revolted, burning and looting the rich man's possessions. The rich looked to the military to maintain order and their way of life. They yielded power to their generals until one rose above them all and grabbed power for himself."

"Yeah. That sounds like us. Give us an opportunity and we'll grab power for ourselves. We don't change much Solomon."

A pair of black wings descended to the ground a few feet from Solomon's side of the board. The crow flapped its wings and cawed. The bird took several large hops towards the chess board and when it came to the edge, lowered its head. With its beak, the crow pushed Solomon's rook into the white piece in front of it. The bird let loose a whooping squawk before flying off to a birch to watch the rest of the game with his friends.

"My rook captures yours on d7," Solomon announced.

"Show off," the man said, suppressing a grin.

"Would you deny an old man his fun?" smiled Solomon.

"No, I wouldn't," laughed the man. "King's rook to d1."

"And in this land," Solomon continued, "an entire shore was not enough to satisfy the newcomers. They needed to push west, to claim more. More land. More resources. More wealth. They drove her keepers off the very land they cared for. And if they did not go peacefully, what did they do? They killed them."

"The opportunity to advance in life, to become more powerful, to make more money even when you have enough, is what motivates us Solomon. More money equals more power."

"Money is a false shade of *power*," said Solomon. "My queen at e7 to e6."

"Yes, I know. But you forget we're talking about my kind. They know nothing about *power*. What they're after is power," said the man. "Bishop at b5 to d7. Say good bye to your rook Solomon. There are two types of people in this world."

"Nay. There are three."

"The haves and the have nots. The rich, we call them the one percent, they control the lives of the poor. They make the rules and we have to follow them. If we don't, we'll find ourselves homeless standing on a street corner somewhere. The rich, they control the corridors of government. The rich control the media. They decide who gets what job. You name it, they control what keeps the world in motion."

"Youth and beauty," interjected Solomon.

"Yes, yes, I know. There is always the exception, but the people at the top..." the man shrugged, letting out a deep sigh of defeat. "If you're at the bottom, you suffer."

"Sounds dismal," replied Solomon.

"It is," returned the man. He paused and added, "Rent, food, clothing. These are life's three necessities. We'll do anything for them."

"You forget love."

"I didn't forget love. Love, and I'm not talking about the sort of love that money can buy, is a bonus if she finds you. Finding true love is rare these days with our preoccupation with power and money. And beauty. No. Rent. Food. Clothing. These are the three necessities that drive us. Some have good jobs, others don't," the man said. "We're either worried about losing them or we're trying to get ahead. We'll do anything to protect what we have, no matter how large or small our share is."

"We put on false faces to show the world because that's what's expected of us," the man continued. "We're supposed to convince others that our lives couldn't be any better than they are, when the truth is, at night, when our faces come off, they reveal the pain we're really in."

"True. Man is afraid to show his authentic self," offered Solomon.

"Or, we'll put on a good front to convince someone that what we're saying is true, telling our little white lies, even if behind it all, we don't believe what we're saying is true at all. Fake it until you make it we're taught. And yet, most of us will never make it."

"We lie, we cheat, we steal," said the man. "All just to get ahead or to stay alive. Whether it's the white collar guy with his smooth gravitas, his refined sense of the truth, or the poorest of the poor who only knows how to survive at the crudest level. The poor. They're the ones most likely to go to jail, for a warm winter coat or for a crumb of food."

"There are no ethics in any of this, no morality. You

either sleep with a roof over your head and food in your stomach or you go without. We're a bunch of wolves dressed in sheep's clothing, willing to tear the clothes off our neighbor's back if it means getting ahead one inch in life."

"We suck up and brown nose to anyone who has something we want. We'll take abuse at work. We'll work longer hours for less pay. And through it all, we put on happy faces because that's what we're expected to do. That's the compact we enter into for keeping our jobs."

"People without are left scratching and clawing to make ends meet. Disparate job opportunities are met with gatekeepers whose qualifications don't measure up to our own. Yet they decide who gets a chance at an opportunity. It's not what you know, it's who you know. We've become keywords printed on a digital page. You're valuable only if you can line a person's pockets with money. But the rich, they don't have to worry. They just keep getting richer. They can buy whatever they want, more than enough to be comfortable. They buy their children access, too. Their children's futures are secure as long as they don't mess them up. We call it nepotism. But for those of us who are on the bottom, we're at the mercy of those on top."

"Life is a competition," the man went on. "We're happy to knock each other down when someone gets too close to what we have or what we want. People protect their families, their homes, their bank accounts, their way of life. You're either an 'A' player or you're nothing. We compete for the fanciest home, a chance to dine at the new 'in' restaurant, to wear clothes with someone's name on it. Heck. People set themselves apart by the shopping bag they carry. To be seen carrying a brown bag from a boutique is somehow more prestigious then a plastic one reading Wal-Mart or Sam's Club. Those who hold the greatest positions of power, those who have the most money, hold the key to a life few will ever know. They're careful who they let in. But give us our bread and our circuses, give us our scandals, sensationalize every message the media feeds us, give us our fifteen minutes of Youtube fame, and we're happy."

Solomon looked on, *feeling* the man's pain.

"Take me," said the man. "Where's my quality of life? I get up at the crack of reveille. I stumble to the shower, shave, have my morning coffee. Then I'm out the door to catch a train. The train, it's crowded. People have little regard for one another. They talk even if everyone around them is trying to salvage whatever small piece of their day they can. They spread themselves out across the seats even if people are standing in the aisle. They go to work when they're sick. They don't care about anyone else. They care only about themselves. They're afraid to miss a single day of work because they're afraid of losing their jobs or a day's pay."

The man looked Solomon straight in the face. "Do you know how many days of work I've missed because some thoughtless, self-centered bastard decided he'd rather grace the world with his germs than stay at home and get better?"

"Too many," responded Solomon, sympathetically.

"Too many is right." The man was gaining momentum. "I get off the train and am greeted by a herd of people. I feel like a head of cattle being moved through the lines of a slaughterhouse. Everyone is bumping into each other, cutting each other off. Sometimes they'll run right into you. Literally, run into you. I've had to brace myself for collisions."

"And if it's raining I have to take the subway. The subway is worse than the train. People cram in. You can hardly breathe. The inside is filthy. People cough in your face, they push you to make room for themselves. Where is the civility? We act like a bunch of animals. Walking is preferable. But the sidewalks, *errrrr.* The people. There are too many of them. Cutting in front of you, clipping you as they walk by. They'll stand in the middle of the sidewalk, blocking traffic, typing insignificant messages to one another because someone has figured out that texts are legal packets of cocaine. People don't care. We're just in it for ourselves. We're all caught up in the same rat race, scared of losing our jobs or our homes or our fancy cars or how we're going to make the next payment on our kid's college tuition. We live in houses of cards we've built for ourselves that can fall at any time. And we accept this as normal. We accept this as though it was right."

"True. Man goes about the business of dying far better than he goes about the business of living," agreed Solomon. "But not all men. There are some who walk this earth who stand firm in truth. There are a few."

"And then at the end of the day, I do it all over again. I'm back on the train and headed home. I look around. No one's happy. They're just as unhappy as when they boarded the train in the morning. We're a bunch of zombies going through the motions. And our weeks? Our Mondays through Fridays? They're blackholes we mark time with."

"Tell me," asked Solomon, "what is this fascination with the palms of their hands?"

"Palms of their hands? You mean cell phones."

"Yes. That must be it. I have watched their adoration for these small things grow. It was not always this way. But now, everyone seems to have one."

"I don't know. Convenience, I guess. Why do you ask?"

"I see them holding them up."

"Oh. They're taking photographs. Probably of you."

"Photographs."

"Yes, photographs. Pictures. They save them to their phones and to the cloud."

"The cloud?" Solomon asked, *peering* into one.

"Not that cloud. Cloud...it's a computer term."

"Saving pictures is a good thing. This way Man can remember how the world once was. If not for their photographs, they might never look up," Solomon said. "But I wonder. Why do men limit themselves to engaging the world from the palms of their hands when there is so much more to see?"

"Solomon. I did everything right. I did what I was told to do. I got my college education. Went back and got a higher degree. But my circumstances. They aren't any better for it. All I accomplished was buying into a big lie. This model, this way of life, it doesn't work for me."

Quietly, in desperate resignation, his head in his hands, tears welling in his eyes, the man said, "Their way of life. It's beaten me down."

"Would you not feel the same way if you were one of your one percent?"

"Yeah, well, I'd sure like to have their problems. I'd take all my money and cash in. Find a place to hide."

"Sounds lonely."

"Maybe, but at least I wouldn't have to put up with all the bullshit," said the man. "As it is I make just enough money to stay afloat. Don't get me wrong, I'm grateful for what I have. I'm very grateful. And my circumstances could be worse. Much worse."

"Yes they could."

"Gratitude before griping. But living paycheck to paycheck, month to month, living in fear that my bank account will read zero at the end of the month, not knowing whether my job will end today or whether I'll have one tomorrow. It's no way to live. How do I make a living when it's not up to me if I have a job? How do I make a life for myself? How do I make a future?"

"Men who possess little are not as helpless as you portray," said Solomon. "Knight at f6 to d7."

"Elaborate please," replied the man. "My queen at b3 to b8. Check."

"Man cannot fear losing what he does not have. Knight takes your queen. A poor man can simply refuse to participate in the rich man's story and write another for himself. His could be a story of abundance. But he is afraid to write that story. Instead," Solomon said, bitterness in his voice, "he colludes with the rich man to bring devastation to us all."

"Solomon?" the man asked, surprised.

"Man eschews being faithful stewards of the Earth in favor of being good stewards of profits. Throughout Man's history, Man has waged war and spilled blood for that which does not belong to him, for that which is only borrowed. Man wages war for the right to pillage the ground," said Solomon, anger rumbling like thunder deep inside him. "He argues over the arbitrary fences he has raised to keep his neighbors from taking *his* resources. Does not the Mother provide enough for everyone?" Solomon asked, his temper boiling over.

"Why then, why must Man hoard what is freely given by her?" roared the old man. "The Mother has provided for Man since he first set foot on the Earth yet Man does nothing to reciprocate his gratitude. Man does not care for the very soul that sustains his life. *She* provides him the fruits of her soil. *She* pours her life giving waters so Man may thrive. But Man takes and takes. He does not give back. He plunders her resources to increase his bottom line. Man's appetite for comforts knows no bounds. His greed places a heavy burden on the Mother. Man demands more from her now than any time in his history. And she speaks to him. She warns him of the consequences of his actions. But does Man listen?" boomed Solomon, now at the height of his fury.

The old man turned his head to the sky, and reaching through the clouds, released his light body. Past the moon and the sun and the stars he traveled. Past nebulas, quasars, and galaxies, blazing through space, straight to the membrane separating the Middle World, the physical world, from the Upper World. And when he reached it, he did not pause, but sped through the layer, piercing it as easy as a bank of clouds. Solomon journeyed into the Upper World, the white world, home to Gods and Angels, past crystal palaces and white mountains, into a pure white sky. High into this other world Solomon flew, higher and higher, and higher still, until he found himself flying through a bright tunnel of light, ascending through heaven, white swirling all around, direct into a blazing white sun, until his flight abruptly stopped and he was face to face with the Light, home of the white matter, the source of Creation, the stuff that dreams are made of.

With fiery white surrounding him, Solomon gathered white matter. And once he had all he could carry, he brought it down through the heavens, a column of star silver blazing behind him still anchored to the Light. He flew down through the membrane, past galaxies and the Milky Way, past the sun and the moon, back into the bonds of Earth. When he returned to his body, he brought the white matter through the top of his crown and deep into his heart. And there he held his dreams for the world.

Solomon continued drawing white matter down through the column, still tethered to its source. Star silver poured down from the Upper World into his heart. Fueled by his ferocious intent, the white matter grew at an exponential rate until it was a miniature white sun. And when Solomon could no longer contain the white magic, he roared, unleashing the energy in every direction, sending waves of pure white light, his dreams of love and peace for the world, for miles in every direction.

Time stood still. A hush as pure as the Light itself descended upon the vale. And for a breathless moment the birds in the trees and critters on the ground, and the people who had come out to play, did not move nor make a sound. The man sat, light all around, floating in a sea of amniotic bliss, drifting on waves of euphoria, an irrepressible smile on his face.

When the light had subsided, so too did Solomon. "There is something you should *hear*," he said, his voice steady and calm. "I would like you to connect with the Mother."

Redirecting himself, the man rubbed his eyes, then his face. He patted down his legs and shifted them. He took several deep breaths to clear his mind. With echoes of bliss drifting in the air, he placed his hands on the earth, one on either side of himself. It did not take long before the man found his way to the twilight. He released his light body letting it slip into the soil. He followed the trees' roots down into the Mother's belly. Deep he went, deeper still, beyond the longest roots, through dark tunnels that carved to the center of the earth until his journey stopped, and he could hear weeping. There a wounded heart lay. The wounded heart of the Mother.

Listen, came Solomon's voice. *Drop deeper and listen. Listen carefully. And learn.*

The man did as Solomon instructed. He dropped deeper, and listened. What he was listening for he did not know. But there he sat, cradled in an earthy silence, the sound, deep and rich and moist, like dark soil, a cool damp surrounding him. Minutes that seemed like a moment passed. A loud horrifying wailing leapt from the pit of the Mother's womb shattering the twilight. Unnerved, shaking and trembling, the man was set to let go and return to his body by the tree when he heard Solomon whisper, *there is something you must see*. And so he held to the twilight, bracing for what might come next.

Beyond the fading echoes of the Mother's crying, images came. The man saw hurricanes targeting populated coastlines, their massive energies locked and loaded, ready to unleash their catastrophic damage. Tsunamis wiped away shores, washing thousands of people into the sea in one giant gulp. The monster waves pummeled nuclear reactors, their cores releasing radiation, their lethal emissions spreading like a plague. And where the Mother could not reach the beaches of her continents, she let loose tornados and earthquakes. Communities stood in the way, helpless, unable to escape their deadly paths. The man saw great blocks of ice crashing into the seas, oceans rising, and cities turning into coral reefs, their millions of people fleeing for higher ground. He saw crops scorched by the sun, withered forests, worldwide famines and global disease, whole species dying one by one, and men and women on hands and knees, children too, clutching their throats, taking their final breaths.

When the images had gone the man came back to himself. He sat, his face buried in his hands, unable to speak, nausea painting the inside of his stomach. When he found his voice, he did not look up, but softly cried, "Oh God. Oh God. What have we done?"

"What has Man done indeed," said Solomon. "It is up to the new generation to lead him back."

"But...but....," stammered the man, tears in his eyes. "We're human. Human nature...."

"Humankind's nature is not to lust after coins he cannot carry home," said Solomon, cutting the man off. "Humankind's nature is of Light and to Light he shall return."

"You're an idealist," the man replied, sullenly.

"If you were not such an idealist, why then are you here?"

Having no answer, the man ended their game, quietly, saying, "Rook to d8. Checkmate."

"Well played," responded Solomon.

The man got up from the ground, brushed himself off, and slowly walked across Summit Rock to the cliff's edge. He looked out over the plateau and into the valley that separated him from his friend, a glacial river running through it. Just below him was The Great Lawn, a magical glade hidden among a forest of towering oaks. Few knew its whereabouts; it was not marked on any trail map. There was the Mall and Ramble — two small forests — woodland paths meandering in each. His eyes wandered upriver to where the North Woods lied, and The Ravine where he could just make out a group of climbers scaling a granite wall. He traced the teal colored river back downstream. Along its banks was Sheep Meadow, the field's tall grasses having turned brown for the season, and on the opposite shore, a little further down, was Strawberry Fields, not named for the wild strawberries that grew plentifully in other places in the valley, but for the wild blueberry bushes, hundreds of them, lining the riverbank, their tiny leaves dressed scarlet for the coming of winter.

The man looked up and down the valley and then across, where Solomon stood, a forest of oak and pine trees dressing his base, his craggy rock face sloping up, his snow capped peak blinding in the late morning sun.

Squinting, the man said, "I cheated."

"Cheating is a matter of perception," replied Solomon. "Was my way not more efficient?"

"I moved one of your pieces. That is cheating."

"You wrote your own story. That is not cheating. That is the way of the Universe."

The man fell silent.

"There is something you need to *see*," said Solomon.

"What is that?"

"The first of our kind. Do you remember what the old crone taught you?"

"Yes."

Solomon silently called to an inhabitant of the valley, and after a brief moment told the man, "He's waiting."

The man nodded.

Letting his eyes wander, the man looked out over the cliff. It didn't take long before he caught sight of a bird surfing the currents and updrafts of the valley. The golden eagle soared, its great wings extended, gliding in large, graceful circles. Acknowledging Solomon's request, the raptor called out in a high pitch, his cry echoing off the old man's massive rock wall.

The eagle plunged out of the sky and like a bullet, ripped through the air, steering a course straight to Summit Rock. When the eagle reached the cliff, he hung motionless, a breeze gently flowing through his feathers. With his wings spread wide he looked straight into the man's eyes.

The man gave the slightest nod of his head and backed away from the cliff's edge. Finding an old oak, the man eased himself down, and with his back against the tree, closed his eyes, the eagle still hovering in his spot. The man cleared his mind and fell deep into the twilight even as the eagle softly chirped to help the man mark his place. With his intention set, the man released his light body into the eagle.

All at once, the man became the eagle and the eagle was the man. All the man's thoughts, all his emotions, everything that made him him, his consciousness, was now in the eagle.

The man felt the eagle's mighty wings, stretched to either side, the wind rolling over and under them, providing the giant bird lift. The man felt his legs — the eagle's legs — dangling freely in the air. Stealing a moment to flex them, he felt the steel pointed tips of his razor sharp talons.

Solomon sent a burst of wind to Summit Rock and before the man could fully adjust to his new home, the eagle and the man skyrocketed upward, riding the gust like a massive wave rolling over the valley.

No longer bound to the earth, the man flapped the eagle's wings as the pair climbed high into the air. The two glided in silence, the only sound the wind rushing through the eagle's feathers, the wind buffeting against the bird's ears. And he and the eagle soared. They roared through the sky, climbing. After a spell, the man leveled their flight path and willed the eagle to bank to the left before tracing a long, slow circle above the valley floor.

Through eagle eyes, the man saw twinkling shards of light cascading all around, prisms of white, landing on the earth like snow, echoes from the Upper World gently floating down. The eagle let out a shrill cry, one of delight, but even as he did, the man saw white threads, glistening, thousands of them, fanned out through the valley; a web of light connecting the vale's creatures, the trees, the river, the hillocks, meadows and glades, and all that was within the valley to each other, Solomon, and the world beyond it, too.

The man, fully in command of the eagle, followed the river to the North Woods, came around and then steered the pair south to Strawberry Fields. They banked to the east and ascended into the sky aiming straight for Solomon's peak. When the man and eagle were face to face with Solomon, the man shared a moment with his friend.

Follow the river, the man heard Solomon's voice in his head. *Downstream.*

The eagle bobbed his head once and the man sent the

pair off, using a ribbon of light from below as their map. The two traced the river's course as it led them out of the valley and into a steep gorge that separated Solomon from another of his friends.

The neighboring mountain and Solomon watched as the man and eagle wheeled in the air before following the river out of the gorge. The pair glided on up currents, the land below passing by at a blazing speed, and when they came to a place where the waterway branched in another direction, Solomon silently urged the man and the eagle to take the way to the right, the man easily guiding the bird's path in the direction Solomon nudged.

Nearly an hour had elapsed into their flight when the man saw that the world around him had changed. Gone was the cloud white of Solomon's valley. A deeper shade of gray had crept in and was beginning to take hold. And in the distance, the man bore witness to a menacing black wall. It sat on the horizon, dark and foreboding, surging into the sky, billowing and roiling as though it were a thing alive.

There is something you must see, Solomon reminded the man.

Not wanting to fly nearer the dark bane, the eagle softly whimpered. But despite the raptor's misgivings the two flew headlong into the coming pitch. Below, the valley's glacial waters had turned a gray mess and the air was quickly filling with gray particles. Struggling to see what laid behind the wall, the man could just make out the outlines of tall buildings.

Suddenly, the eagle pulled up, bucking, resisting flying further. The man tried to impress his will upon the bird but the eagle refused to comply.

There is something he must see, Solomon said to the raptor.

Reluctantly, the eagle relented, and with long, grudging

flaps of his wings continued towards the seething, dark wall. The river was flowing a heavy gray and the air was filled with a fine, sooty haze. The buildings had turned black, and a demonic city had risen up to meet the sky.

The man steered their flight higher.

From their new vantage point, the man saw that the city was enshrouded in a threatening, pulsating black and above it, sinister clouds swirled. Black cords, growing ever longer, stretched out from the city in every direction. The river was running with a thick sludge and the closer the river flowed towards the city, the darker and thicker the waters became, black cords swimming upstream, churning the waters black.

Exactly when it happened the man couldn't say for sure but the eagle warned him. The sooty haze had turned into a dense, black fog, speckling the eagle's wings with a fine, almost black powder that weighed heavy on their flight. Toxic ebon fumes steamed from the ground, the noxious vapor choking the bird. The eagle reared, hacking and retching amid the stench. The man sought to impress his will upon the eagle but the dark fumes had become too much for the bird, confusion and ataxia having set in. Desperately, the man tried to assert his will upon the bird, wildly flapping their wings, struggling to stay in the sky, but there was nothing he could do. Overcome, unable to tell up from down, the bird and the man spiraled out of the sky, convulsing as they dropped, even as the city's black cords slithered up into the black soup to meet them.

Helpless, the man stared into the oncoming jaws of the black tendrils as they tumbled to the earth.

A mighty blast of wind rushed from Solomon's heights, across the lowlands, straight towards the dark city. It howled through the gray lifting the man and eagle into the sky, away from the black arms, carrying them high beyond the black fog where the eagle could breathe once more. Safely above the macabre disaster below, the raptor regained his easy form.

A little further on, asked Solomon of the man and eagle.

The pair ascended on royal wings where the air was cleaner. With the world far below, the man saw the dark city, a pulsating, ominous blot. It appeared as a beating black heart, healthy and strong, spreading a black malignancy that smothered the life out of everything it touched. The land surrounding the city was scarred with areas that were in various stages of decay, though pockets of beauty remained, the largest, Solomon's valley. And far into the distance, spreading its own death into the world, the man could make out another city, just as dark and malignant as the one below him.

The man looked straight down. His heart almost gave out. The black cords, like dark serpents, were attacking the web of Light, coiling around the glistening white strands, strangling them, pulling and tearing them apart, waging a vile war. In and around the city, the black manacles were winning. Large sections of the gleaming web had been destroyed. And in their place, the serpentine strings were building their own web, black and hideous, an evil, a vehicle for delivering destruction to the world.

Not far from the city, where a proud mountain once stood, a tumorous black mass stained the landscape, black cords and the dark cancer having overrun it. The mountain was there but it wasn't there, a horrifying void disfiguring the earth, dead, not alive.

"The first of our kind," said Solomon.

Overcome with revulsion, the man doubled over and emptied the contents of his stomach to one side of the oak tree.

"What?" the man asked coming back to himself, re-membering the horrors he had just seen.

"Even mountains die," Solomon responded, sadly.

"What? What have we done?" the man broke down in heavy sobs.

Solomon let the man cry himself out. When the man was done, through tear-stained eyes he pleaded, "Is there no hope?"

"Yes. One fragile line bears Man's hope," the old man re-minded his friend.

"But how? How can there be hope in the face of that?" the man asked, pointing past Solomon towards the distant horizon. "Oh God. We're doomed...doomed...doomed...." the man repeated to himself, his head in his hands, half out of his mind.

Softly, Solomon responded, "Doomed? Not doomed. There is always hope."

"Yes. Doomed," the man persisted. "How can there be hope?"

"Earthkeeper, how can we mountains not have hope when there are those like you among us."

The man looked up at his friend, anguish tearing him apart, tears streaking his face, and quietly asked, "But what can I do?"

"As much as any mountain can," Solomon answered. "As much as any mountain."

About the Author

Scott Bishop was born and raised in northern New Jersey, earned his Juris Doctor from Syracuse University College of Law, and is licensed to practice law in New York State. He currently resides in New Jersey where, when time permits, he pursues his passions for the outdoors, photography, cooking, and writing.

Scott is the author of *A Soul's Calling*, a memoir about a man who listened to his heart instead of reason. *A Soul's Calling* is set in the rugged but enchanting Himalaya where mountains speak and nature is imbued with a special kind of magic. A modern day adventure, *A Soul's Calling* weaves the timeless themes of living an authentic life, the consequences of power, and what a man would do for unrequited love.

FOR MORE INFORMATION, VISIT THE WEBSITE
WWW.SCOTT-BISHOP.COM